For Janet Lily Sislowitz
—J. Y.

For my friend, Abby
—D. A.

SIMON & SCHUSTER BOOKS FOR YOUNG READERS • An imprint of Simon & Schuster Children's Publishing Division • 1230 Avenue of the Americas, New York, New York 10020 • Text copyright © 2012 by Jane Yolen • Illustrations copyright © 2012 by Derek Anderson • All rights reserved, including the right of reproduction in whole or in part in any form. • SIMON & SCHUSTER BOOKS FOR YOUNG READERS is a trademark of Simon & Schuster, Inc. • For information about special discounts for bulk purchases, please contact Simon & Schuster Special Sales at 1-866-506-1949 or business@simonandschuster.com. • The Simon & Schuster Speakers Bureau can bring authors to your live event. For more information or to book an event, contact the Simon & Schuster Speakers Bureau at 1-866-248-3049 or visit our website at www.simonspeakers.com. • Book design by Chloë Foglia • The text for this book is set in Garamond. • The illustrations for this book are rendered in acrylic paint.
Manufactured in China • 0812 SCP
2 4 6 8 10 9 7 5 3 1
Library of Congress Cataloging-in-Publication Data
Yolen, Jane. • Waking dragons / Jane Yolen ; illustrated by Derek Anderson. — 1st ed. • p. cm. • Summary: In the morning dragons wake up, tumble out of bed, and get ready to fly into the sky. • ISBN 978-1-4169-9032-1 (hardcover) • [1. Stories in rhyme. 2. Dragons—Fiction.] • I. Anderson, Derek, 1969—, ill. II. Title. • PZ8.3.Y76Dr 2012 • [E]—dc22 • 2010037058

first edition

WAKING DRAGONS

by JANE YOLEN

PAINTINGS by DEREK ANDERSON

2012

Simon & Schuster Books for Young Readers
New York London Toronto Sydney New Delhi

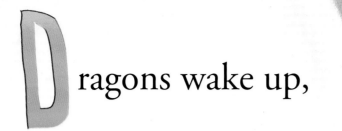
Dragons wake up,

dragons rise.

Dragons open
dragon eyes.

Dragons blink,
dragons bumble,

dragons leap,
dragons tumble
out of bed

to brush their teeth,
the fangs above,
the fangs beneath.

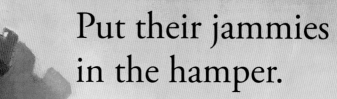

Put their jammies
in the hamper.

Then all dragons
skip and scamper

down the hall
on four big feet
to the kitchen
there to eat

breakfast waffles,
topped with syrup,
which makes dragons
really cheer up.

Wipe their faces,
runny noses,

get into their
outdoor clothes-es.

Kiss their dragon
mom good-bye.
Leap from cave
into the sky,

where dragons
get to fly.

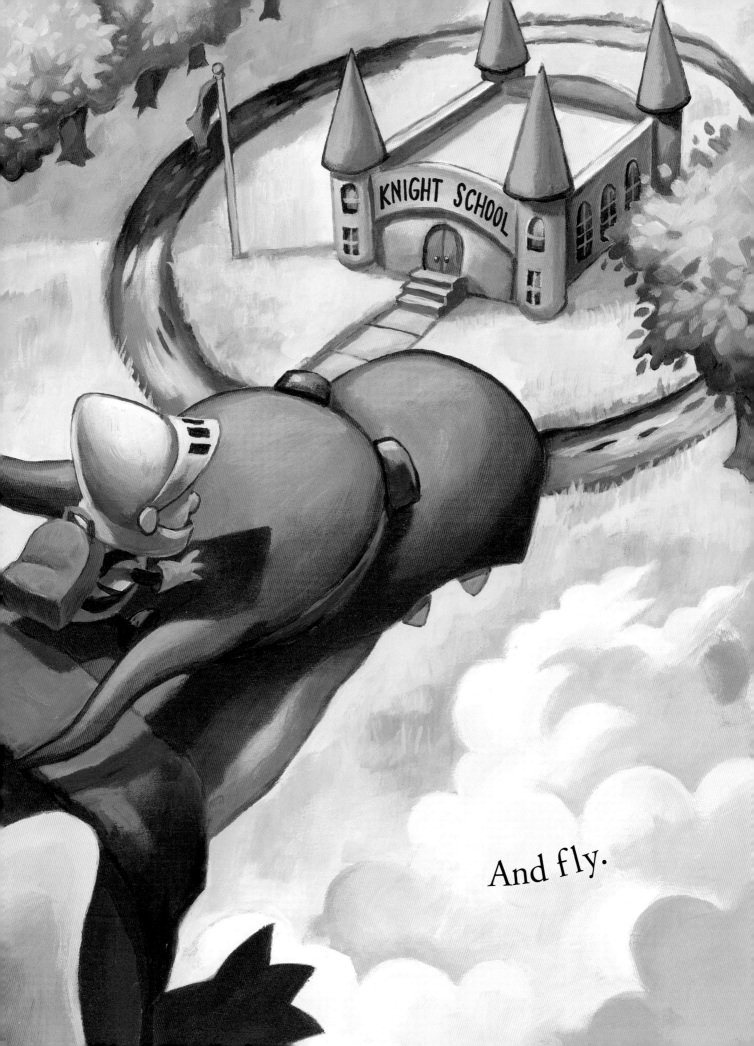

And fly.

And fly.